HILL OF FIRE

An I Can Read Book®

HILL OF FIRE

by Thomas P. Lewis

Pictures by Joan Sandin

HarperTrophy
A Division of HarperCollins*Publishers*

For Dinny

Hill of Fire
Text copyright © 1971 by Thomas P. Lewis
Illustrations copyright © 1971 by Joan Sandin

Library of Congress Catalog Card Number: 70-121802
ISBN 0-06-023803-8
ISBN 0-06-023804-6 (lib. bdg.)
ISBN 0-06-444040-0 (pbk.)
First Harper Trophy edition, 1983.

Once there was a farmer

who lived in Mexico.

He lived in a little village,

in a house

which had only one room.

The farmer was not happy.

"Nothing ever happens,"

he said.

The people in the village
thought the farmer was foolish.
"We have everything we need,"
they said.

"We have a school,

and a market,

and a church with an old bell
that rings on Sundays.
Our village is the best there is."
"But nothing ever happens,"
said the farmer.

Every morning,

when the farmer woke up,

the first thing he saw

was the roof of his little house.

Every morning for breakfast

he ate two flat cakes

of ground corn.

His wife had made them

the night before.

He put honey over the cakes,

and drank cinnamon tea

from a clay mug.

"Nothing ever happens," he said.

10

It was still dark and
the farmer got ready
to leave for the field.
His son Pablo was still asleep.
"Perhaps today," said his wife,
"something will happen."
"No," said the farmer.
"Nothing will."
The farmer led his ox away
and did not look back.

At night the farmer returned.

He fed his ox.

Then he sat down by the fire.

Pablo played with five smooth stones.

He threw the stones at a hole

he had dug in the earth.

"See, Papa!" said Pablo.

"I got one in!"

But the farmer was tired.

He did not answer.

Every day was the same.

15

One morning

the farmer woke up very early.

He pulled on his woolen shirt.

He took his big hat

from a peg on the wall.

"I must go to the field early,"

he said.

"The plowing is not done.

Soon it will be time

to plant the corn."

All morning the farmer
worked in his field.
The ox helped him.

When there was a big rock

in the way, the ox stopped

and lay down.

The farmer pushed the rock away.

"Tst-tst!" said the farmer.

The ox looked at the farmer.

Then the ox got up

and pulled again.

Late in the morning,

when the sun was high,

Pablo came to the field.

"Pablo!" said the farmer.

"Why are you not in school?"

"There is no school today, Papa,"
said Pablo.

"I have come to help you plow."
The farmer smiled.

He reached into his pocket,

and gave the boy

a small wooden toy.

"A bull!" cried Pablo.

The farmer had made it for his son

during the hot time of the day

when he rested from his work.

Pablo helped the farmer

plow the field.

The ox pulled,

and the plow turned up the soil.

Suddenly the plow stopped.

The farmer and his son pushed,

and the ox pulled,

but the plow did not move.

It sank into the earth.

It went down,

down,

down,

into a little hole.

The little hole became a bigger hole.

There was a noise

deep under the ground,

as if something big had growled.

The farmer looked.

Pablo looked.

The ox turned its head.

White smoke

came from the hole in the ground.

"Run!" said the farmer.

"Run!"

There was a loud CRACK,

and the earth opened wide.

The farmer ran,

Pablo ran,

and the ox ran too.

Fire and smoke came from the ground.

The farmer ran all the way
to the village.
He ran inside the church
and rang the old bell.

The other farmers came
from their fields.

People came out of their houses.

"Look!" said the farmer.

"Look there!"

That night no one slept.

Everyone watched the fire in the sky.

It came from where the farmer's field
had been.

There was a loud BOOM,
and another, and another.

Hot lava came out of the earth.

Steaming lava spread

over the ground, through the trees.

It came toward the farmer's house.

It came toward the village.

Pieces of burning stone

flew in the air.

The earth was coughing.

Every time it coughed,

the hill of fire grew bigger.

In a few days

the hill was as big as a mountain.

And every few minutes

there was a loud BOOM.

Squirrels and rabbits ran,

and birds flew away from the fire.

People led their burros

and their oxen to safety.

Pieces of burning ash flew everywhere.
The farmer and his neighbors
put wet cloths over their noses
to keep out the smoke.

Some of the people

went close to the steaming lava.

They carried big crosses.

They prayed for the fire to stop.
The farmer and Pablo watched
from the side of a hill.

When the booming stopped
and the fires grew smaller,
the farmer's house was gone.

The school was gone.

The market was gone.

Half the village was gone.

One day some men in uniform came
in cars and trucks.

"So you are the one with the plow
that opened up the earth,"
they said to the farmer.
They laughed.
"You are lucky to be alive, *amigo*."

The soldiers looked at the village.

"Everyone must go!"

the captain said.

"It is not safe to live here any longer."
The farmer and his wife and Pablo
and all the people of the village
went with the soldiers.
They rode away in the trucks.

The farmer found a new house.

It was bigger than

the one they lived in before.

It was not far from the old one.

But it was far enough away

to be safe from *El Monstruo*,

which means "The Monster."

That is the name the people gave

to the great volcano.

The people made a new village.

They made a new school

and a new market.

They had a great *fiesta*
because now they were safe.
At the *fiesta* the band played,
and the people danced
and clapped their hands.

People from the city came in a bus
to see *El Monstruo*.

The people of the village
sold them oranges and melons
and hot dogs and corn cakes to eat.

Now the farmer had a new field.

Every morning he woke up early.

It was still dark,

and *El Monstruo* glowed in the sky.

Every morning for breakfast

he ate two flat cakes

of ground corn.

His wife had made them

the night before.

The farmer went
to his new field.
His ox went with him,
just as before.

Sometimes Pablo brought

the children of the village

to see the farmer.

From the field they could see

the volcano smoking,

like an old man smoking his pipe.

"Can you make another

hill of fire?"

the children said.

"No, my friends, no, no,"

said the farmer. He laughed.

"One hill of fire

is enough for me."

AUTHOR'S NOTE

This story is based on reports of the eruption of Parícutin volcano on February 20, 1943. It came up in the Mexi-
can state of Michoacán, in the cornfield of a Tarascan
Indian named Dionisio Pulido.

No one was killed, but more than two thousand people
are said to have lost their homes.

Only once before in recorded history has the birth of a
volcano been seen by human eyes. This was on Tenerife,
in the Canary Islands.

People may visit Parícutin today. They will see the
volcano, and also the abandoned village — buried under
many feet of hardened ash and lava.